MALINDA MARTHA MEETS
MARIPOSA

A STAR IS BORN

Written by Marcia Trimble

Illustrated by John Lund

Special thanks to the community of Pacific Grove, California.

For readers interested in reading about the fascinating mystery of the Monarch migration, including the Monarchs East of the Rockies who migrate to Mexico as well as Monarchs like Mariposa who are born West of the Rockies and migrate to California, the following sources are listed as a reference.

The Monarch Habitat Handbook by Lincoln P. Brower, Mia Monroe, and Katrin Snow ... available from the Xerces Society Tel 503 232 6639/FAX 503 233 6794

The Monarch Butterflies of Pacific Grove ... available by calling the Monarch Habitat Restoration Committee Tel 408 648 3100

The Great Butterfly Hunt by Ethan Herberman, published by Simon and Schuster, Inc. 1990

Publisher's Cataloging-in-Publication
(Provided by Quality Books, Inc.)

Trimble, Marcia.
    Malinda Martha meets Mariposa : a star is born / written by Marcia Trimble;
    illustrated by John Lund.
    -- 1st ed.
    p. cm.
    SUMMARY: Faced with writing a story about summer vacation,
    Malinda Martha imagines herself directing a backyard theater
    performance of the metamorphosis of a monarch butterfly.
    Preassigned LCCN: 98-94132
    ISBN: 1-891577-57-3 (hbk.)
    ISBN: 1-891577-58-1 (pbk.)
    1. Butterflies—Juvenile drama. 2. Butterflies--Metamorphosis--Juvenile drama.
    I. Lund, John (John H.) II. Title.

    PZ7.T734Mal 1999   812'.54 [E]
    QBI98-1590

10 9 8 7 6 5 4 3 2 1

Text was set in Century Schoolbook and Lemonade.
Book design by Nutshell Design, Inc.
Printed in Hong Kong by South China Printing Co. (1988) Ltd. on acid free paper. ∞

The story of Mariposa, the Monarch butterfly
is dedicated to the hundred million Monarchs
that migrate to their warm wintering sites each year,
sometimes sites up to 4,000 miles away...
the only migration that is considered
"an endangered phenomenon" by the International
Union for the Conservation of Nature...
and to the caring people who have sought protection
for the Monarch through legislation, private funding
for volunteers to tag the traveling Monarchs, and the
creation of ecological preserves and tourist paths.

The chalkboard reads:

September 8th
Welcome back to school!
Teacher – Miss Claus
WRITING ASSIGNMENT
"Summer Vacation"

Malinda Martha smiled. The faces of her sunflowers were brushing against her cheek.

"Thank you for planting us when we were little seeds and watering us until we could peek through the ground and drink showers of sunlight and grow toward the sky," they whispered.

Malinda Martha's eyes opened wide ...
a curtain of sunflower faces was falling
before her. Her backyard was bursting
into a stage!

A hummingbird hovered over the stage.

Backyard Theater Auditions

"Will you fly back and hum for the star of the show?" asked Malinda Martha.

A ladybug flew by.

"Your talent is feeding on mealy bugs and aphids and spidermites," said Malinda Martha. "There is no role for you. Fly away, ladybug."

A snail crawled onto the stage.

"There is no role for pests," said Malinda Martha. "Crawl away!"

A grasshopper
hopped onto
the stage.

"Go lay your eggs along
the roadside.
Hop away, grasshopper."

A mole ran onto the stage.

"Your talent is eating on bugs and earthworms," said Malinda Martha. "You are good at eating larva ... and roots of plants, too. You need a set designed with a tunnel or an underground runway. There is no role for digging. This is not the show for you. Run away, mole."

A ground squirrel scurried
onto the stage.

"You cannot burrow into the show,"
said Malinda Martha. "Go find a tree
to climb, with roots and bark to gnaw
and nuts and fruit to nibble on. There is
no role for you. Scurry away, squirrel."

A butterfly fluttered by and dropped a speck on the leaf of a plant ...

... and Mariposa made her debut as a wee tiny pale green egg clinging to the fuzzy underside of a tasty milkweed leaf ...

ACT
I
EGG

Waiting to become a Butterfly

pale green egg that was clinging to

tiny

wee

the

from

hatched

it

the fuzzy underside of the tasty

milkweed leaf

... as soon as

A tiny caterpillar ate its transparent shell ...

The caterpillar munched on the milkweed leaves to the hum of the hummingbird ...

from the wee tiny pale green egg that was clinging to the fuzzy underside of the tasty milkweed leaf ... after eating its transparent shell as soon as it hatched

Waiting to become a Butterfly

The caterpillar munched its way
across the leafy stage ...
performing the leading role in
ACT II ... an eating machine.

The caterpillar munched ...
and grew ...
and shed ...
and stretched ...
over and over again until it molted*
five times.
The cast of characters ran in from
backstage ...
just as the caterpillar was wriggling
out of its old tight skin.

Malinda Martha clapped.
"Good timing!" she shouted.
"The speck has grown as big
as my thumb"...

PRODUCER
DIRECTOR

green   egg   that   was   clinging   to   the   *fuzzy* *underside* *of* *the* *tasty*

... munching on the   leaf   milkweed

Waiting to become a Butterfly

its

of

out

wriggling

and

stretching

The caterpillar bowed low into ACT III hanging upsidedown from the stem of the milkweed leaf ...

"Look at the clever caterpillar," shouted Snail and Hummingbird.
"See its larval skin shrivel up from its head to its tail and fall off," laughed Ladybug.

eating its transparent shell as soon as it

hatched from the wee tiny egg

"It doesn't have any new skin this time," cried Grasshopper.

"It looks like limey green chewing gum," said Squirrel ...

"painted with a splurge of gold dots," added Mole.

"It's a magician!" bragged Malinda Martha. "Did you see how it slipped out of its skin without falling off the stem?"

that was clinging to the fuzzy underside of

Waiting to become a Butterfly

growing to full size stretching and wriggling out of its old tight skin munching on milkweed leaves after eating its

transparent shell as soon as it hatched from the wee tiny pale green egg that was

leaf attached to the silken thread it made with the sticky liquid from its spinneret*

PUPA*

"Look at the pupa! The soft cover is drying and hardening. The dots are coming out of nowhere. Look how the shiny green chrysalis* is shimmering"...

clinging to the fuzzy underside of the stem of a milkweed leaf ...as it hangs upside down from the tasty milkweed

Waiting to become a Butterfly

The curtain closed at the end of ACT III. The caterpillar disappeared inside its private dressing room leaving the cast in suspense, having to wait ... during a long intermission ...

INTER-MISSION

thread it made with the sticky liquid from its spinneret growing to full size stretching and wriggling out of its old tight skin munching on

milkweed leaves after eating its transparent shell as soon as it hatched from the wee tiny pale green

from the caterpillar hanging upside down from the stem of a milkweed leaf attached to the silken

egg that was clinging to the fuzzy underside of the tasty milkweed leaf ... while the pupa shimmered from its splurge of gold dots changing.

Waiting to become a Butterfly

On the twelfth day of camping out and observing, Malinda Martha and the cast noticed a change.

ACT
IV
ADULT

"Look, the chrysalis turned from limey to grey green ... and it's becoming transparent," they exclaimed. "See the orange and black wings," they cried out. "Look, the pupa's splitting open! See the head! And the legs!" they shouted together.

"The butterfly is pulling free from the pupal shell," Malinda Martha announced.

"A Star is Born!
Meet Mariposa, the Monarch Butterfly!"

Malinda Martha and the cast watched the finale. They glued their eyes to Mariposa's wet crumpled black veined wings and saw them expand as she prepared to flutter away.

"Encore," they shouted.

She showed off her wings trimmed with white spotted edges as she glided over the milkweed plant. They applauded and waved goodbye as she floated off the stage to sip the sweet nectar in the flowers and begin the migration south to her overwintering site.

"Safe journey, Mariposa!" they called out. "Safe journey," echoed Malinda Martha. "Fly to California. Fly to Pacific Grove. Fly to the eucalyptus trees in the Monarch Grove Sanctuary."

Malinda Martha was celebrating this miracle of metamorphosis* with the cast ...

BEST
ACTOR
CATERPILLAR

BEST SOUND
EFFECT
HUMMINGBIRD!

BEST DIRECTOR
MALINDA
MARTHA

MIRACLE OF
METAMORPHOSIS
LIFETIME AWARD
MARIPOSA

... when Miss Claus's voice interrupted the thoughts fluttering through Malinda Martha's head and jolted her back to the classroom.

"Time to share your stories! Who will go first?" asked Miss Claus.

VOCABULARY LESSON

larva - caterpillar
pupa - resting stage
molted - shed its skin
spinneret - silken thread maker
chrysalis - protective shell
metamorphosis - change in form

Malinda Martha sighed. "If only a Monarch had left an egg in my backyard, there would be so much to tell. But ... next summer ... Mariposa's great great grand butterfly-child might fly the last leg of the return trip to Boise and flutter over the milkweed plant in my backyard" ... *so there could be a wee*

Malinda Martha raised her hand.
"Miss Claus, I'd like to go first," she said.

leaf

milkweed

a

of

underside

fuzzy

the

to

clinging

egg

green

pale

tiny